CW00745713

Nature's Magician

Anthony Cropper

route

First Published by Route 2009
PO Box 167, Pontefract, WF8 4WW
e-mail: info@route-online.com
web: www.route-online.com

ISBN (13): 978-1-901927-38-2

ISBN (10): 1-901927-38-5

Support:
Priscilla Baily, Julia Cropper, Ian Daley,
Isabel Galan, Manuel Lafuente, Emma Smith

Cover Design:
Martin O'Neill

Printed by Biddles Ltd

A catalogue for this book is available
from the British Library

Route is an imprint of Route Publishing Ltd and is
supported by Arts Council England

Nature's Magician was commissioned as part
of a project called *Writers2Readers* which
was supported by the following organisations.

East Midlands Public Libraries Working together to Promote Books and Reading

Contents

For Stanley

Introduction

'The sound of the story is the dominant sound of our lives.'
Reynolds Price

A couple of years ago I was talking to an old fisherman. He was sitting on a bench by the lower lighthouse, the one that's now a tourist information centre. The tide was out and it was a quiet day. Stretching across the bay, bank after bank of black-green and purple mussel bed. When I was a child, and dared to swim in the sea, those mussel beds used to cut into our feet. They hurt, but we still went there, knowing.

The old fisherman had a big seashell in his hand and now and then he'd raise it to his ear and listen. He had a tough, rough, weather-beaten face. He had small glassy eyes, the whites turning yellow but the blue still clear and fresh.

After a while he passed the shell to me and I too listened to the sound it made.

'It's acoustics,' I said to him. 'It's echoes of the noise that surrounds us. It's not the sea. People think it's the sea, but it's all this, all this sound in the air that gets amplified. It gets concentrated into this shell and it echoes on into the ear.'

The old man looked at me.

'Is that right?' he said.

We talked some more and I told the man about something that had happened to me. The story was true. It had happened only the day before and had left me amazed, stunned, heartbroken.

'I don't believe you,' he said.

'It's true. It happened. I'm telling you.'

'But it doesn't sound convincing. You want me to listen to you? Convince me,' he said. 'Give me something to believe in.'

He told me some stories and after a while I asked why he lied so much.

'Do you want me to drown?' he said. 'Go on. Tell me a story, make it a good one, make it a lie.'

Nature's Magician

My father was in the front room speaking French to a new friend of mine. He was up to his old tricks, asking the time, asking her name, asking how she was.

'Bonjour. Quelle heure est-il?…'

My friend was good company and she listened well. She helped him with his French then listened to stories of when he was at sea.

'We caught a basking shark and had to raise it up on the winch to get it out of the net.'

That one always came out when someone sat with him. After the French, came the story of the basking shark, about how its tail snapped off when they raised it into the air.

I was in another room, in search of a grand unified theory, one to explain the mistakes I'd made, one to help me understand the chaos I called my life. Of course, a grand unified theory was beyond me, but I was never one to give up hope. Drop me in the

Pacific, three thousand miles from shore, I'd still swim.

How much choice in the construction of our universe?

After my universe fell apart my only answer was to lie. I lied to everyone about what happened. My wife had had an affair, two affairs. One lasted a month, the other lasted two years. She said she'd had a few one night stands, but she said that they didn't count.

'Besides,' she said. 'I was probably drunk and can't even remember enough to regret it myself, so why should it bother you?'

One afternoon, when I was a teenager, I almost drowned. I was in the swimming pool, seeing how many underwater turns I could perform. My friend managed nine and I'd vowed to beat it. I counted eleven, twelve, thirteen, fourteen, and when I attempted to stand up I became dizzy. I tried to find the bottom of the pool, panicked, kicked out and luckily, surfaced, gasping, frightened beyond belief.

'Seven,' my friend said then laughed. 'You did seven.'

He was the same friend who stole from my mother's purse, who stole from my brother's money box. The same friend who stole from his father's jacket pocket. He was the same friend who beat up a stranger, a young child, in order to blood his new boots. He was the same friend who did everything in his power to destroy everything I had.

Once, I saw a programme about experiments on animals and benefits to humans. A small monkey with wires attached to his shaved head stared out of the screen.

'If I press this button, he lifts his right hand. If I press this button, he lifts his left hand.'

The monkey did as the man said, first raising one hand, then the other.

My wife asked some crazy questions. One night, she sat in bed and said she wanted to know if lightening was a solid, a liquid or a gas. Another night she wanted to know if it was true that the soul had weight, that water had a memory.

'I'm fifty-five percent water,' she said. 'How much of me will you remember when I leave? What's a flame? A solid, a liquid or a gas? Why is water so unusual? Why is it the only substance to expand as it freezes?'

'I don't know. I don't know. I don't know.'

'Because if it didn't expand it would sink. There'd be no icebergs. Ice would sink and all the ice would go to the bottom of the oceans and it'd never thaw. It'd just collect, get thicker and thicker till all the oceans were ice and there'd be no liquid left anywhere. That's why it expands, because it *has* to expand. If it didn't expand we wouldn't exist. If water didn't have these ridiculous properties then we wouldn't be here. I'm fifty-five percent water. Did I tell you that?'

In another experiment a chimp was sitting in a cage with her baby. The experiment was designed to illustrate something of human behaviour. It was meant to show how people would do anything to save themselves. The floor of the cage was made of steel and, slowly, over an hour, the floor of the cage was heated. The floor became so hot that the mother lifted the baby and held her off the floor, she jigged from one foot to another, keeping the foot off the metal, trying to cool it down before switching feet again. At some point, the floor became so hot that the chimp had to make a decision. Did she lie down and die, letting her baby rest on top of her in order to survive? Or did the mother stand on the baby and save herself?

'Electricity,' said my wife. 'Now what's that? Solid, liquid, or gas?'

She was in tears, it was four in the morning. It was

the closest I'd come to sleep in three days.

'Belief,' she said. 'It's all a matter of belief.'

One time, sometime, I was in the kitchen with a hammer and a nail. I was trying to puncture an aerosol can so I could fill it with water and use it as a water pistol. I was only six, or seven, or eight. Really, of my age, I've no idea. Another time I was at the light switch, turning it on and off, trying to see the edge of light, trying to beat it across the room. I thought, if I had a camera I could quickly take a picture and get the edge of light, have a picture; half light, half darkness.

I remember my first day at school. I remember walking through those big blue wooden doors. The first painting I did, the sky was white and the clouds were blue. The teacher shouted and told me to look out of the window.

'Numbskull.'

I got tangled in a net on the docks and was almost pulled forty feet onto the back of a stern fisher. One night I was almost killed in a fight. Once I was chased by a drunk in a car. He tried to run me down and twice I was pulled from his path.

There's these and there'll be other occasions I'll never know anything of. How many seconds from disaster?

I had a recurring dream where a tidal wave pulled me into the sea and I drowned.

My father was a fisherman and many times I'd been to sea.

'Why would anyone want to do this for a living?' he said.

I really have very little idea about his life. He spent over forty years at sea. He told me a story about a man who put his finger in the hole on the side of a winch. The winch was used to pull tonnes of fish, miles of nets and cable. This man put his finger in the hole and when the winch turned it took off his finger. My father stuck it back on and headed for shore. Two days later they arrived.

The sea has been a big part of my life. I was brought up by the sea and my relatives, as far back as I know, were fishermen.

If the story had a beginning, what happened before then?

I'm still working on this grand unification theory.

What are the possibilities? What's the circumference of imagination? What's the area of an idea? How can we measure anything at all? How can I get closer to the far side of a memory?

I had an idea for a story. It was about a father and a son.

Here.

One foggy night the son is out collecting wood and becomes lost. The father goes to look for him but he falls down a hole and descends into a hollow world. The father initially searches for a way out, but, after some time, he gets used to the new world, a world where he is applauded everywhere he goes, treated like a king, a saviour. The son is left on the surface and grows old searching for his father. One day, the father is out walking and he hears the voice of his son. The son is crying, saying that he's lonely without him, that he wished his father would return. The father looks up and sees the hole through which he fell. He has the choice: does he climb out and go to see his son, his family, or does he stay in the other world?

The trouble is, Father, the trouble is, is that the people who live there, in this hollow world, they're not real, none of it's real, it's all in the man's imagination. The people who applaud and clap and cheer, they're not there.

He stays, of course. And out of guilt and loneliness, the son kills himself. But the father, he never once regrets his decision. He never knows what actually happens. He can't see the real world because of the illusion he's created. That's the tragedy, the inability to accept the world which was his.

Water is an amazing substance. Find something else that exists freely as a solid, as a liquid and as a gas. Find something else which we use so much. Find something else that expands when it cools. Find something else to drink, to cook with, to swim in.

My father spent his life at sea.

I grew up by the ocean.

One thing I'm good at is skimming stones. Give me a body of still water and a handful of flat stones and I'm away. There. Look. See how we skim over the surface?

One two three four five six seven...

The story has no beginning and no end, and, if we use imaginary as opposed to real time, neither do we.

One time I was sitting in the shed at the bottom of the garden and my four-year-old son came out to talk to me.

'Why don't you come and play?' he said. 'Come back to the house.'

'I'm already in the house. I'm in the kitchen, you go and look.'

'Are you?'

'Yes.'

He ran off to the house, taking the longer way, through the conservatory. It gave me enough time to make it through the back door. When he arrived in the kitchen I was standing there, leaning against the side, reading a newspaper.

'You are,' he said. 'Come and play.'

'Okay,' I said. 'What do you want to play?'

My wife asked some crazy questions.

'Why did we ever get married?' she'd say. 'How much of me do you remember?'

The Carpenter

1.

The barn was big and in the winter, cold, and in the cold the carpenter worked more quickly. Part of the roof was loose and on rainy days water would seep into the far left corner of the room. The carpenter kept his wood and his tools away from the damp. He'd worked in the barn for seven years and at least once on each day he'd considered repairing the roof. But, that would cost money and would take time. Commissions came in, but the money he received was barely enough to pay the rent on the barn, the rent on his room, and pay for tools, food and materials.

The barn was directly north of the town, visible from almost any point; a compass for all who'd become lost.

2.

For two weeks the carpenter had been working on a small bed. The bed was for a leading figure in the town whose wife had been taken ill. The woman's condition was serious and the man had wanted something for when she returned from hospital. He'd wanted the bed making quickly, but he'd also wanted it to be beautiful.

'It may be the bed she dies in,' said the councillor. 'The doctor gave her no more than six months. I want the bed to be carved with cherubs and angels. Do this quickly for me, carpenter, and I'll pay you well.'

3.

The carpenter had himself been ill with a fever, yet he'd worked on despite the bouts of shivering and sweating. The bed was to be ready for Friday and the carpenter worked all night to finish the face of an angel. As dawn broke, his chisel slipped and gashed his finger. Blood ran over the bed, across the figure. The carpenter washed his hand in a bucket of water then wrapped the cut with a bandage he'd made from the sleeve of his shirt. He wiped blood from the angel then completed the carving. That done, he lacquered the bed and sat on a stool. A moment later the barn door opened and the councillor was standing before him.

4.

'Time to rest. Maybe I'm paying too well.'

The councillor inspected the bed. He crouched down and ran his hand over the frame. The wood was sticky and the councillor sighed.

'There's a stain,' he said. 'On this angel's wing.'

The carpenter explained that the stain was in the wood, that he'd tried to remove it, that the stain would not come away.

'It's deep into the grain. Maybe it's meant to be.'

The councillor stood and faced the carpenter.

'I asked for the bed to be ready. The frame is still wet. How can my wife sleep in this when she returns tonight? This was meant to be a surprise. And that stain. I was told you could work wonders with wood. You disappoint me, carpenter.'

The councillor turned and left the barn and the carpenter stood alone. His hand ached from the gash and he pulled the bandage tight. The money the councillor left was not enough for rent and food so he decided to move his belongings into the barn.

From now on, he would eat, sleep and work here.

5.

An hour passed and two men came to collect the bed and when the bed was gone the barn seemed strangely empty. All he had was his bench, a few tools, a lathe and a stool.

Tomorrow, thought the carpenter, I'll patch that roof and fix the windows. If I'm to live here, it will need to be warm.

6.

The carpenter walked to town, paid the arrears on his room and collected his blanket and belongings. On his way up the valley he called in at the wood suppliers.

'Merchant. All I have is this. I need food, but I need wood for my work.'

'You're in luck, carpenter. Tomorrow sees new stock and I need to clear space. Give me all you have and you can take that oak, that pine, that sycamore. That's more than three times what you'd normally receive for the price. Make the most of the offer, carpenter. If you don't, then tonight, the wood will be burned. Don't turn away from a profit.'

The carpenter gave the merchant the rest of his money and began the long walk to his barn. He knew the route well, but his eyes were poor and now and again he stopped to rest.

7.

When he returned, his stock room held more wood than ever. The merchant had been true to his word, the wood here would last him well. All he needed now were commissions.

The carpenter checked the wood, closed the gate then made a bed from hay. He lay down, covered himself with his blanket, and, though shivering with fever, he fell asleep.

8.

Dreams are often stronger in a fevered mind and in his fevered dream an angel came to call. The angel appeared as a bright white light and the carpenter was sure he was not lying on hay, sleeping, but was wide awake. He felt warmth run through his body as the angel leaned forward and touched him on the forehead.

The carpenter woke and gazed round the barn. It was dark and he could barely see the outlines of his tools, his lathe, the stock in the corner.

The carpenter was fond of the dark and the quiet. If he was warm, he could lay still and allow his mind to drift. At night he often thought of Marianne, a young woman who worked in the grain store. She had long dark hair tied in plaits and always had a warm, pleasant smile. She was always kind and happy with the carpenter whenever he walked by on his way to town. But, he thought, she was probably kind and happy with everyone. Why should she pay him any favours? He was just a carpenter and the town had many important people. She will marry a rich man, he thought. A man who'll provide for her.

For a short while the carpenter remained awake, then, he pulled the blanket up over his shoulders and fell asleep.

9.

It was not long before he was dreaming again and in this second dream he saw himself at his bench, working away at a piece of wood. The wood was bright gold and though the carpenter looked hard, it wasn't clear what it was he was making. In the dream he hovered high in the barn and as he slowly descended the carpenter at the bench turned and looked up towards the roof. The golden wood was bright but the carpenter saw that he himself was old. His skin was pale grey and his face gaunt.

This time, when he woke, the carpenter was shivering. He sat up, his breathing heavy. Now, the dark in the barn was threatening, the shadows and tools becoming monsters and ghosts. The blackness appeared to shift around him. The wood store was a dark prison, the gate opening and closing as shadows flickered on the wall.

The carpenter pulled the blanket up to his chest and wrapped his arms around his knees. He told himself that there was nothing to be afraid of, that it was just the illness making his dreams appear so real.

He displaced his thoughts by thinking about his work, about the new stock, about sharpening his tools, about mending the roof. After a while he lay back down and fell asleep.

10.

The third dream came quickly and in this a voice talked to him, telling him that he must make something from his last piece of wood. In the dream, he asked over and over what it was he needed to make.

'Only you know what you need to make,' said the voice.

'But it's my last piece of wood. No one will just walk by this barn and buy something I've made on a whim.'

'You must do what you feel.'

'But how do I know?'

'Put your heart into the wood,' said the voice.

11.

The carpenter woke. His finger ached but the fever seemed to have left. He lay still and watched darkness turn to day. After laying still for an hour or more he got up, ate some bread, drank a cup of water then went to the wood store. Only one piece of wood remained. His store had been robbed in the night.

That's it, he thought. The light, the voices. He must have heard the thieves, maybe even seen their torches but was too delirious to act. Maybe they'd held him down and clubbed him?

He lifted the piece of sycamore. 'What use is this?' he said. 'What use are you?'

He flung the piece of wood back into the store and went outside. The sky was clear and blue and from his position he could see down the valley, across the river and into the trees at the edge of town.

'What difference would it make if I ended my life?' he said. 'I have nothing and no one in the world.'

12.

Even when the carpenter was young he showed the attributes of a master craftsman. He would take time with models, had the patience to follow instructions, was careful with tools, would look after things well. He was precise, thoughtful.

At school, he would produce the most carefully constructed pieces of furniture. The teacher would show them round the various year groups, showing what could be produced, given the determination and care to do so.

All that was a long time ago. Almost a lifetime ago.

The carpenter was born in the small town in the valley. When he was seven his father died in a milling accident. His mother took employment with the church, cleaning, but when he was twelve she became ill and died from pneumonia. The boy moved in with the church leaders and was given the opportunity to work with wood. The boy learned fast and was soon helping with tables and chairs. He took his time, smoothed the wood with care and the church carpenter was pleased with his efforts. One afternoon, he was working, finishing a piece, when he heard a voice from behind. He looked round quickly, just as the master carpenter was walking by, carrying wood. The edge of a piece of yew caught him in the face, and even after receiving help from doctors, he lost the sight in one eye. The head carpenter had felt sorry for the boy and helped him while he recovered.

After a number of years the carpenter saved enough to start on his own. The barn out of town was the cheapest he could find and he'd begun with enthusiasm. The years passed and his enthusiasm waned. Each time he produced work he was left with almost nothing. He ate poorly, lived in a cold room, and had nothing to show for all these years of work.

The carpenter had no idea that, on this earth, he had a brother.

13.

The carpenter was gazing down the valley when a man appeared at the gate. It was rare for someone to make the trek out from the town and this man was not someone he recognised. Of course, the carpenter did not know the man was his relation. To him, he was someone who'd taken the wrong path, someone who needed help and direction.

The carpenter brushed his hand over his chin and greeted the stranger.

'Are you lost? The town is that way. Follow the river to the woods. The path takes you.'

'No. I'm not lost,' said the man. 'I've come to see you.'

The man entered through the gate and stood before the carpenter. He was a small man, older, with a tiny white beard. His eyes were clear blue and his skin smooth for his years.

'I need something making.'

The carpenter responded quickly, tired of the hunger and the cold.

'I need you to pay in advance. I'll tell you that now. Last night, my store was robbed and I have nothing left. If you want something, I'll need the money to buy the wood.'

'They took everything?'

'I was sleeping. The first night I slept here and see what happens.'

'Do you consider yourself to be a lucky man?'

'My luck is gone, stranger. No. I'm no lucky man. There's another carpenter in town, by the church yard. Perhaps he can help you.'

'But I wanted *you* to make something for me. It has to be. Have you nothing left?'

'They took all but one piece.'

'Then use that.'

'But what is it you want? You've no idea about the wood, whether it's large or small. What do you want me to make?'

'It's a present. Just make me something beautiful.'

'A box, a trinket box?'

'If that's what you think the wood will make, then fine.'

'But what size. For rings? Money? Papers?'

'The object will speak for itself.'

'And how much will you pay?'

'I'll pay you well, carpenter. But it needs to be ready by tomorrow.'

'That's impossible. You've given me no dimensions, no design, no outline. I'll have to draw it out, cut it to shape, smooth, polish. That all takes time.'

'Then miss some of the stages. You can do this for

me, I know you can. Last night, I had a dream and in the dream I saw a carpenter who lived in a barn out of that town there. In the dream a voice spoke to me and said you could help, that you'd know what it was I needed. The voice said to trust you and if ever a dream speaks to me like that I know I have to listen. I'll return tomorrow, in the evening. I trust you, carpenter. You won't let me down.'

The man turned and walked back out of the gate and headed up the valley. Within a moment he was out of sight and the carpenter sighed heavily.

'I need a miracle,' he said.

14.

The carpenter held the lone sycamore in his hands.

'What is all this strangeness, this talk of dreams? Can you hear me, wood? Will you talk to me?'

The carpenter ran his hand over the length of wood. It was almost a foot in length with a knot and slight kink coming halfway.

'I make tables, chairs, window frames. I make coffins, beds, cabinets. What use are you, sycamore? What use are you?'

The carpenter tossed the wood onto the patch of grass before him and went back inside to search for remnants.

'There's this broken frame,' he said.

He went behind the lathe but all he found were shavings and cuttings.

'Maybe you, bench. Maybe I could fashion you into a table.'

He looked around the room. Thirty-seven years old and all he had was before him.

'What am I to do? Rent and payments on tools. My belly aches from hunger. Is this all I have to show for my life? Cuttings and shavings, hay for a bed, drinking from a bucket.'

The carpenter crouched down on the floor, his head cupped in his hands.

'Think, you damn fool. Maybe this stranger will pay you well. Just make something, anything. What do you have to lose?'

The carpenter went outside and searched in the grass till he found the sycamore. He took it back inside, sat down on the straw and began to work with his knife.

15.

Waking dreams come in many forms. Sometimes you take a walk then wake at your destination, unaware of your journey. Sometimes you stare out of a window, allow yourself to drift, and wake ten, twenty, thirty minutes later. You feel you've been away yet are unable to recall the details of where you've been. The carpenter was not used to these waking dreams. He was a practical man, led by his belief that given the time and the tools, he could produce high quality work.

'I live. I make things. And that is all there is.'

Whether it be the muse, the ghost within, the mind working in desperation, his ill health and tiredness, whether it be none of these did not matter for the carpenter worked without stopping, without thinking about the outcome. He smoothed the surface, worked away at the knot, the bend. He followed the lines in the wood, removed weaker areas. He continued through the night and on into the morning. Time had stretched or shrunk or stopped or had ceased to exist, because the following afternoon he felt a jolt and realised he was still sitting on the hay, the wood in his hands. He glanced towards the door and realised it was late afternoon. Though he'd worked with wood for years the skin on his hands was sore. He'd worked differently, more closely, more delicately. The skin on his tips of his fingers was worn smooth, his palms were red from twisting and turning the wood.

16.

The day slipped away as the carpenter worked once again. As the light began to fade he suddenly woke from his trance and gazed towards the door.

'He won't come. Lies, broken promises, lies, hollow dreams.'

The carpenter dropped the wood to the floor and walked outside. Long rose-tinted clouds edged slowly towards the horizon.

The carpenter waited. He gazed toward the gate as darkness fell.

'I should never have trusted him. I should have used the wood for a fire, for a club, for a stake. I should have used the wood as a marker for my grave. Here, once again, truth rests in another day of waste.'

The carpenter took a drink of water, went back inside and climbed beneath his blanket.

17.

Not even man has a soul, he thought. The dreams I dream are just dreams. The real is here, in this barn, fashioning wood into chairs and tables. The real is here, in the cold in my hands, in the cut on my finger, in the hunger of my stomach. If God exists, then He has made my hands cold and my stomach ache. Why didn't He wake me when the thieves were in the barn? Why did He let me sleep, let me dream of angels, let me see myself old and cold and worn by the years? What good was that? Was He on the side of the thieves? Was He keeping *them* warm, making *them* rich, making *them* smile and be happy? And there was I, sleeping through it all.

The carpenter raised his voice to the sky.

'There is nothing here or there. The stars are just stars. The sun is just the sun. The rain falls and comes into this room. The wind blows through that broken window and I work with wood. I make things that people buy and with the money I receive I try to live. I've paid my way but it has always been a fight. Why am I kept hungry and cold? Why has there never been a moment of pleasure in my life? Thirty-seven years old and my skin is worn and my body aches. I believe in nothing. Do you hear? I believe in nothing.'

18.

Though the cramps in his stomach were strong, the carpenter slept. The night had turned cold. The wind blew from down the valley and every so often the aromas of food floated in the air, the sound of voices rested on the wind. The carpenter rolled over and pulled the blanket tight to his chest. His head throbbed, his eyes ached, his dreams were dark and violent.

When he woke, he opened his eyes and he was blind.

19.

With simple acceptance of his fate, the carpenter sat on the bed of hay and expected death to follow.

'I am gone,' he said. 'Now, I know I have no means to make money, to work with wood, to pay my way. What use am I in this world? A blind man whose cold and hunger brings him close to death.'

The carpenter sat still for an hour or more then as he went to move he felt the sycamore by his feet. He raised it up and ran his hand over the surface. It was rougher than he'd remembered. Had he not already smoothed it?

The carpenter ran his hand across the wood as he waited for death to bring him down. After a while, he took out the knife from his pocket and began whittling. He began in the centre, taking out large pieces, then moved to the top, rounding. He worked once again at the centre, this time more carefully, feeling the bend, as though it were a hip.

20.

The carpenter had no conception of how long he'd been working. He took a sip of water and as he fumbled for his blanket he felt the presence of someone in the room.

'Who goes there? There's nothing to take. The tools are worthless, the wood store is empty, my clothes are tatters. I have nothing, see, I have nothing.'

The carpenter heard footsteps.

'Please. My eyes, I'm blind. Leave me to die in peace.'

The carpenter could hear breathing.

'And were you blind when you carved this?'

'There's nothing. What little I had in this world has been taken from me. Everything is gone.'

'And what have you left?'

'I've nothing. I don't even have a soul. The heat from my body disappears. My stomach shrinks. My desire to live has all but gone. What have I left?'

'And what if I took this, this wood you carved.'

'Take it. But please, leave me. Consider it a gift from a dying man.'

'You've seen this?'

'I've no desire to see the mess I created.'

'And what do you want?'

'Want? What do you mean?'

'If you could have something, in exchange for this. What would you want?'

'Who are you?'

'Are you afraid?'

'Everyone is afraid.'

'Who do you think I am?'

'I think you might be the man who promised to return. I think you might be a passer-by, a thief. You might be the person who robbed me of my wood. You might be a messenger, telling me my time on this earth is finished.'

'And what is it you want?'

'Want? Please, stranger. Don't taunt me. Why ask now what I want?'

21.

You take a man, one you've thought about for weeks and months, even years. You put him in a barn, away from town. You make him feel his loneliness. You make him poor, you make him hungry, you see him lose his possessions. You mention that he has a brother about whom he knows nothing. You talk about the loss of his mother and father. You take away his eyesight. You take away his hope. Then, you think, how can I make him suffer? What more can I do?

You introduce a woman who has always loved him but has never told him. You offer a glimmer of hope, but he finds all this out after she has married. You introduce the possibility of escape. You bring work, but that goes awry. You bring friendship but that turns to hate and betrayal. Why have you invented this man? What scapegoat is he? Why do you want to see him suffer? What is it you're trying to show?

Do you wish to see him triumph over adversity or do you wish to see life's trials grind him down? If he is beaten, why is the story not about the victor, about his character, about his search for glory?

What is laid bare by your words?

22.

For four years I've tried to end this story and no real end comes to mind. I tried telling the story one way, then another. No use. No end seemed to fit, no end seemed appropriate. I tried ending with the beginning, ending with multiple endings, ending with a surprise, a twist, with the expected. It seems some stories have no natural conclusion.

I'm one of eight children, the youngest. I've six sisters and one brother. Am I writing about our contact, or lack of contact?

I tried an ending where the writer died and the story was never complete.

I tried an ending where the carpenter died.

I tried an ending where a brother arrived, where the earth ceased to spin.

The real truth: no end was ever discovered, and in this, the carpenter became immortal.

Of All Things

My brother was seven years older and by the time I was born he had his own life.

Give me the child to seven, so the saying goes, and I'll give you the man.

The last time I saw him was in hospital. He was in a coma and his face was bandaged. A narrow window left his eyes visible but even they were closed. I sat by his bed, feeling like an intruder into his space.

We'd not seen each other in seven years, not spoken for almost as long, never sent cards or birthday wishes, we just got on with our lives, knowing that we both existed, but neither willing to make a move to talk or visit. He worked on the south coast for a communications company and had made his way into management. He'd been divorced for five years and had no children. As far as I knew, the lack of offspring was the reason for divorce. His ex-wife, Alison, had been desperate for children but none had arrived. Again, what little I know is that she now has a child, a girl, and she lives in France.

Our parents died when we were fairly young and I'm my brother's only surviving relative. I sit here, now, in his room, unsure of what to say. In truth, I feel I hardly know the man. We grew up together but were separated by our age difference. He was always distant, somewhere on the horizon, always through a window, going out, visiting friends, away camping or on school trips. And here we are now, forced together again.

Doctors rarely give any false hope, and this one told it as it was, giving all possible outcomes.

'He may survive, yes, but he could be brain-damaged, he might not walk, he might have a weakened heart...' The list went on and I wondered how it was possible for one man to have so many complications.

'So, it doesn't look good.'

'The internal injuries alone were severe.'

The doctor had a trimmed grey beard and wore thick-rimmed glasses which mirrored my reflection. He seemed way past retirement age but was still clinging to work. He'd had a lifetime of situations similar to this; giving bad news to the hopeful. What a terrible burden, I thought. All those tear-filled eyes. Mothers and fathers desperate for their children, desperate for this man to give them something to cling to. Words now spoken as matter of fact. These are the injuries, these are the possible outcomes. If A then B. If B then C. My brother seemed to have the alphabet.

'He may never recover from the coma.'

The journey to the south was six hours by car. I'd stopped at the services and called in the shop to buy snacks: drinks, crisps, chocolate. The shop had gifts and I wondered if there was anything I could take for my brother. It struck me then that I hardly knew him. I didn't know his taste in music or books, didn't know what clothes he wore, whether he liked football or cricket. I didn't know if he joked and laughed or was serious, contemplative. Did he drink? Did he smoke? Was he religious? How much had he changed over the years?

I looked around the shelves. All these terrible gifts, all these things and nothing suitable.

Simon had been on his own in a room for two days and by some miracle, someone, somewhere had found my number. Of all things, I'd been cleaning the windows, something which I'd never done before in my life. I heard the phone, climbed down from the ladder and was told the news.

I found Simon with wires to his chest, a drip in his arm, a tube up his nose. At the far side of the bed was a screen with four moving lines, differing colours, all frightening in their acknowledgement that Simon was still alive. For a while I just watched the screen, expecting a peak or trough, a continual loud bleep or cessation of all activity.

What do you do? What is there to do? Is it him awake and me asleep?

A nurse entered and noted down some information from the screen. She went to the window and straightened the curtains. She nodded at me and smiled.

'He'll be glad you're here.'

Of course, her saying that made me worse. I felt like a fraud, sitting here, feigning concern. Truth was, I was finding it difficult to know how I felt. I didn't know what to say or do, didn't know how to act, didn't know what to feel.

'Thank you.'

'Have you talked to him? It's okay. You can hold his hand, and talk. Some people are put off by all this, they think they need to stay away from the bed. Please. Push the chair up, don't be afraid. He'll be glad to hear your voice.'

'Is there anything I can do? Keep an eye on the machines? I could...'

She glanced at her fob, smiled, then left the room.

So there we were, together in our loneliness. I sat back in the chair and felt guilty that I hadn't done as the nurse asked. If he could hear, then maybe he was waiting for the sound of the chair being moved, maybe he was waiting for me to hold his hand. Could he hear? What would he want? Speak, brother. Tell me what I should do?

On arrival at the hospital I'd been given a briefing of his injuries.

'I'm afraid his clothes had to be cut away, all we found were these.'

The man handed me a small box which contained a wallet, a set of keys and a watch.

I sat with Simon for an hour, not saying a word beyond my initial hello and I was thankful when the doctor entered and asked me to leave. They needed time to take a closer look at his injuries.

'Get some sleep. Come tomorrow, whenever you like. I'm sure you've spoken enough for the night.'

Another feeling of guilt quickly rose within me.

'Would you mind signing this? Check his details and sign, please.'

I said goodbye and looked into the tiny window

which exposed his eyes. They remained closed, lifeless.

'I'll see you tomorrow. Take care.'

As soon as I said that I felt ridiculous. What must the doctor think, me telling a man in a coma to take care? He's suffered horrific injuries, is fighting for his life, cannot even hear or see.

'Sorry,' I said to the doctor. 'Please. I don't know what I'm saying. You must think I'm a fool.'

The doctor jotted down some notes and glanced at me.

'Huh?'

'Saying that.'

'What?'

'Sorry. I'll go. I mean. I'm in the way. I'll go.'

Simon's flat was different than I'd anticipated. The place was a complete mess: pots and pans in the sink, unwashed plates on the table, takeaway cartons on the side. The TV had been left on, lights blazing, toilet used but not flushed.

This wasn't my brother. He'd always been tidy, close-shaven, showered, always scrubbing his fingernails, his bedroom had everything tidied away, toys in boxes, all stacked neatly. Everything had its place, shirts and trousers folded, but now, clothes spilled over drawers, the laundry basket a mountain, towels strewn about the floor. And there was a smell, not terrible, just something reminding me of slightly stale food or over-ripe fruit.

It was a small flat: one bedroom, sitting room, kitchen and bathroom, located on the sea front, at the top of an old hotel. The entrance was grand, but the building itself had fallen into disrepair. These may once have been decent dwellings and maybe some still were. But this, like I say, was different than I'd expected.

The window in the sitting room was the biggest surprise, it being totally false. When I first entered I thought he had a sea view, but no, the frame and view were just painted onto the wall. Curtains hung to the side, but this, this was bizarre. The only true window was in the kitchen, situated three or four feet to the left of the sink. It was a small square window, maybe three feet wide and it was open when I entered. I had to lean out, across the worktop, stretch as far as I could in order to pull it closed. And the view? It looked directly across to the sloping roof of the other side of the hotel, slates that were almost within touching distance. Leaning out, to the left, the side of the hotel and a small car park, to the right the gully between roof tops.

I picked up some of the rubbish from the floor,

folded the towels and placed them over the radiator, pushed clothes back into drawers and closed them. I filled the sink and scrubbed at the pots and pans. I kept on at it for hours till the rooms were spotless, all the time pushing away thoughts of when we were young.

'Do I have to take him?' he'd say to our mother.

'He's your brother, you can at least act as though you like him.'

And off we'd set, him in a mood, stroppy with me for pestering to go.

'But he's just a kid.'

'And he's your brother. If he doesn't go, *you* don't go.'

When he left home I was nine going on ten. I never understood why he left so young. It was seen as being unusual, for him to take a flat just half a mile away and work in town. After he left he rarely came to visit. I never had the courage to ask if there'd been an argument, never picked up on anything, never heard raised voices or felt tension in the air, but, whatever, he left and the distance between us increased. After a couple of years he moved further away, first twenty miles and then not long later to the south coast where he stayed. Mother never went to visit, wasn't even invited to the wedding. He married in a registry office and sent a card, telling us of the news, saying as some form of justification that he'd not wanted for us to bother, that it would have been a big journey to make for such a small occasion. He sent a photo of the ceremony, just Simon and his wife with two other people and an old man, presumably Alison's father. Mother kept the photo on the sideboard for a week but then it was vanished away and even after she died I never came across it in her belongings. Simon had been in a coma for two days, but, in reality, as far as I was concerned, he'd been in a coma for years, we both had, the contact we had could not approach closer to zero.

Of course, now, I felt guilty for not trying harder. Would it really have been that difficult to ring and ask how he was? Would it have been hard to at least try for some connection, for some communication?

I used to tell myself that being brothers didn't mean any more than being friends or colleagues. We shared the same roots, but that didn't necessarily mean I had a stronger bond to him over anyone else. Why should I ring just for the sake of it? I should want, not feel burdened. All fine justification for laziness, for apathy, for forgetfulness, for fear. And yes, maybe there was some fear, fear of making the first move, fear of ringing, fear of saying hello to a relative stranger who happened to be my brother. In my mind, we had little or nothing in common. We had nothing to discuss. If I or he rang, it would be awkward and would leave us feeling insincere, hollow, inadequate. Maybe tomorrow, maybe next week, maybe next year.

We change and remain the same.

I finished tidying the flat and sat on the sofa. I wondered if he'd be pleased with what he saw or whether he'd say why, why did you tidy my space? Can you not see I prefer chaos? What gives you the right to come here and put order to my world? You think being my brother gives you some insight into what I want? Am I wrong to live like this?

In the morning I woke on the sofa. It was after nine and I couldn't believe I'd slept so long. I was still dressed in the same clothes, not even finding time to take off my shoes. I'd had a heavy, tar-like sleep and it was still lingering on my forehead, still pulling my eyes to close.

I was apprehensive about returning to the hospital. I checked the phone for messages but there'd been none. Before leaving I glanced over the flat, opened the fake curtains and switched off the lights. I was about to leave when I remembered the kitchen window. I'd opened it again when the stale air was getting to me.

I leaned over the worktop to pull the window closed but stopped to look again at the view. To the left, the small car park devoid of any vehicles. Out to the right, a slate-lined valley ending at an iron rail. Then, I noticed, along the roof, toward the end of the gully, a ladder. Lord knows why, but I pulled myself through the opening and stepped out onto the roof. The gully was about five feet wide, twenty feet high, maybe a hundred feet above the street. I climbed the ladder and once at the top saw the roof was edged by a small wall. Over the far side, a tall chimney and at the base of the chimney an old wooden stool. As I walked towards the chimney I was overwhelmed by what I saw. The view across the bay and out to sea was spectacular. There was nothing between me and seemingly endless space. Not another building could be seen. All before me was immensity: a limitless, still blue sea.

I sat there for some time, ten minutes, maybe longer, and as I was about to leave, noticed a crevice between the bricks in the chimney. In the crevice was a small brown envelope and in the envelope a photograph.

I had no recollection of when and where the

picture was taken but it was of the two of us, when we were young.

I'm with my brother and everything is black and white. We're both dressed in shorts, his hair's standing up on end and we're wearing big old football boots. My arm's linked with his and we're about to cross a road. My brother's chest is puffed out, as though he knows I'm remembering him, as though he knows I'm seeing him through all this impossible space. My face is dirty and he's holding a coat in one hand. The street behind us is empty, the buildings are tall and are filled with windows reflecting sunlight. There's nothing and no one in the world beside the two of us. When I look close I see I've mud on my legs and I'm wearing football socks. One of the socks is pulled up, baggy round my knee, the other's hanging down over the top of my boot. My brother's grey jumper is tucked into his shorts and his smile is huge. I love him. Yes. I see and feel it clearly. Just look at us then and look at us now.

Then I remember a kicked ball and shattered glass. I'd wanted to run, to hide, to avoid confrontation, but he knocked on the door and apologised.

Listen, brother. There's things I'll never know and never understand.

For a moment I close my eyes and when I open

them I'm standing on the edge of the building, looking over to the sea. The sky's bright blue and I've a feeling I want to take a leap into the void.

Once, we were young, and the world was not too bad. My brother was and always will be with and of me and I know that in the end there's nothing but acceptance.

Today I'll go to the hospital. I'll sit by his side and will hold his hand and will tell him all I can remember about when we were young. I'll tell him why I always wanted to go with him and why I'd admired and looked up to him. I'll tell him all this and more. I'll tell him about my life, about what I like and dislike. I'll tell him about the view from his roof and I'll laugh as I tell him about my incomplete memories of our olden days. I'll tell him about how I'd wanted to phone, about how I'd hoped all along that *he'd* call. I'll tell him about our mother, about how she'd cried when she received the photo of his marriage, that she'd cried because she was happy. I'll tell him about anything that comes into my mind, about how I tidied his flat, about the takeaway cartons, about false windows and broken glass. I'll tell him about everything, and when I run out of things to say, I'll tell him some more, too.

Totem and Taboo

'She always passes the same time every day. She gets to that corner, that's where she does it.'

It was 12.45 and we were at Mark's, just opposite the playing fields. We'd been listening to 'L.A. Woman' and Jim Morrison was beginning his *Mr Mojo* frenzy. We had it loud and when people walked by they looked up at us.

Bort came down the street, bag over shoulder, blazer hanging loose, a pair of dirty old jeans that seemed too long for her. When she reached the corner she took a skirt from her bag, rolled up her jeans then pulled the skirt over the top.

'They don't let you take them off,' said Mark. 'It's the rules. She's not had them off for six months, sleeps in them, all sorts. They christen them, too. They must reek.'

Winter or summer, Mark's house was always hot. His mother and father left the heating on thirty and if ever they needed to cool down they'd open windows. There's times I'd been at his house and no one could move for the heat. Friday nights we'd rent three or four videos and watch them one after the other. Sometimes we'd stay up and watch them twice.

'It'll never catch on,' I'd said. 'Who wants to watch films at home?'

Horror, thrillers, all sorts. A video shop opened in town and after a few years we'd been through the most of them.

'She's looking at us. Fuck, she can see us.'

'I'd take them off,' said Mark. 'She's had three abortions, not even left school and three abortions. They said if she has another she'll be sterilised. She's with that big guy, the one with the Triumph. Slag. Have you seen the size of him?'

Sometimes we'd watch so many films I never knew what I'd watched. Once, Mark found some of his father's porn collection in the loft. There were things on those I'd not even dreamed of, more frightening and more real than anything in the movies. I never looked at his father the same again.

'You get stripes, red stripes, brown stripes, all sorts of stripes. There's all sorts of ceremonies and initiations. You know what the red stripe's for?'

Bort looked at us again then tossed the bag over her

shoulder. She was old for her years but there was a child still in her eyes, too.

'You should see them,' said Mark. 'Unbelievable.'

Bort flashed a V sign then continued on her way to school.

'Slag,' said Mark. 'Three fucking abortions.' He poked three fingers into the air and thrust them at her.

One time I was at Mark's and it was so hot no one could move. We'd watched two films, had eaten popcorn, crisps, peanuts. We'd been sitting for hours, watching Charles Bronson hunt the people who raped his wife. After that we watched *Friday the 13th* and I knew I'd be taking the long way because I was too scared to cut through the fields.

'Imagine a UFO landing out there,' said Mark. 'They might bust into the house and whisk us away. They might take us and say, *We want to see how you earthlings make love. We have a hundred women and you will only be set free when you've been with all of them.* Imagine.'

On the piano was a family photograph. Mark looked at the photograph then at me.

'The dirty fucker,' he said.

We left his house and climbed over the fence into the school field. The spikes were high but we'd been over a thousand times.

'One kid slipped and got pranged,' said Mark. 'He

got one right here and that was that. If it happened to me I'd top myself.'

Years ago we pushed pins into our fingers and swore to be blood brothers.

'I'll never change,' said Mark. 'This is me forever.'

I read sailors once nailed flags to the mast to show they'd never surrender.

In the bushes we found an old crash helmet. It was a big heavy thing with red stripes down the side. It had no visor and Mark pulled it over his head.

'Hey, do you think she'd fuck me if I wore this? I'm a fucking Hells Angel. Fuck fuck fuck. Brumm brummm.'

Mark removed the helmet and when we got to the rugby posts I said, 'Watch this.'

I swung the helmet back and forth, aiming for the top, somehow knowing everything would work out.

'No chance. You'll never do it.'

I lobbed the helmet into the air and it landed right on the post. It balanced there, looking out towards the school like some kind of totem.

When we got to the class all the younger kids were up against the windows, their desperate faces filled with the desire to know.

'Look at that fucking helmet. Look. Who the fuck put that there? Look.'

The helmet stayed right to the end of term and then came the long summer holidays. It was a hot summer, sweltering hot. We watched a lot of films and talked about UFOs coming in the fields to whisk us away. Nothing much really happened. And by the end of everything we were still the same, the same but a little older.

This is My Life

At the beginning of the month I went to a wedding. It was in a small church in a tiny village and we arrived just after the bride. Embarrassing, yes, but we slipped in at the back and before long the ceremony was in full flow. The groom was an old friend of mine and we'd not seen each other in eight years. Eight years. Neither of us could believe it. Eight years. We kept saying it to each other and we promised not to leave it so long again.

The wedding was excellent. My friend was overcome, but managed to hold himself together for the afternoon and evening. He admitted that the day before, in rehearsal, he'd been in tears, in fact, he'd been uncontrollable.

It was a fairly large wedding, maybe a hundred and fifty people. It's hard, in some ways, being the focus of all that attention, being at the point of all that good will, hope and love.

'I might look calm,' he said. 'But inside me is a raging storm.'

My own wedding was very small, just seven of us. It took place eight years ago. Eight years. Time doesn't pass, it's all here, now, with me.

My friend is forty-four years old and he's at the beginning of a great new adventure. He's changed, of course, from when we were young, from when we were going out together, drinking, talking of the future, wondering where we'll be and what we'll become. I wish him well. On his wedding day I'd never seen him look so happy.

Last week, I caught my wife in the garden with the neighbour. He had his hands all over her and when I confronted them he initially said he'd only touched her back.

'I was just saying goodbye,' he said.

When I questioned him further he admitted to venturing to other regions and he apologised. My neighbour's wife said it was due to lack of attention from his mother, that he found it difficult to deal with friendly relationships and often overstepped boundaries.

When I asked my wife about what had happened, she said she hadn't known how to fend him off, that she wasn't in any way involved, that it had all been unwanted attention.

'I just didn't know what to do,' she said. 'I'd been meaning to tell you.'

I probed further, and, finally, it emerged that the two of them had been seeing each other for almost eight months. We had a terrible forty-eight hours. We talked, sulked, argued, ranted, shouted and cried. I ended up in a mess. I was physically and emotionally wrecked and inside me, too, was a raging storm.

On the day before I caught them I'd been thinking about how lucky I was. It's very rare for me to have thoughts like that and now I can't help but think it was an omen.

Well, there you go.

My wife decided to leave but the neighbour decided to stay with his wife and family. This morning, I received a postcard from Antigua. My friend had found time to write and wish me well.

'Let's meet when we return,' he said. 'The four of us.'

My life is composed of all these things. Being alone can be difficult and I won't deny I'm finding it hard.

Of course, I'll not phone my friend. I'll leave it eight years or more and next, when we meet, we'll all be that much older.

I'm hoping to see him the same, still shining with

light for his new bride, still raging inside with all that great undying love.

Crocodiles

There are three people in this story:

Roger: mid-thirties, casual appearance, stubble, Texas Longhorns T-shirt.

Jimmy: young child.

Mag: late thirties, dazed, attractive, slim. Has the look of a gangster's moll.

The story begins downstairs of a bay-windowed terrace. The rooms have at some time been knocked into one, there's a chair and sofa, a small kitchen with a tiny breakfast bar and two stools. A mirror over the mantelpiece, a television in the corner. By the wall near the window, a long tubular hoover. Behind the sofa, a few empty cardboard boxes. Pots and pans dry on the draining board. On the side next to the sink bottles of red and brown sauce, a large tub of salt, a bottle of vinegar. The room is very plain and has the look of a tired rented house. We join the story in the month of April.

Part One

Jimmy is sitting on the hoover. In one hand he holds two small white candles. Roger is by the window. He holds the curtain to one side and looks along the street, first one way, then the other. To the left, the end of the street backed by a brick wall some thirty feet high, to the right, the crossroads. After a moment he lets go of the curtain, walks to the table and lifts a glass of water. All the while, Jimmy is very still. There's a long silence then Jimmy speaks.

'Sometimes I sit like this, like a statue, and I don't move anything, not even my eyes. Did you see I was a statue?'

'I thought you'd gone quiet,' says Roger.

'I was a statue. Sometimes, I'm a statue when I'm in bed, and I can hear my heart going boom boom boom.'

Roger smiles and takes a sip of water.

Jimmy holds up the candles.

'Can we light these? You said we could light these when the power's gone.'

'When it gets dark. I said if this power cut lasts, when it gets dark, yes. Remember, they might fix it by tonight.'

'Yes, but can't we close the curtains?'

'It'll still be light. Wait till it gets dark, when it gets dark we'll need them. If we use them now then tonight we won't have candles. And don't sit on the hoover, please.'

'Can we watch the telly?'

'The telly's not working. It's electric. There's no electric to make the telly work.'

Jimmy stands up, looks round the room and sees Roger's reflection.

'The mirror's still working.'

'It is, yes, but that's not electric. It's not the same. We've been through this. The mirror's different. That's me, there, when did you see me on the telly?'

'When will it get dark? I want to light the candles.'

'Later. After your mother's back.'

'Simon's got two bouncy castles and a huge blow-up swimming pool.'

'You told me.'

'Can we get two bouncy castles?'

'When you get a bigger garden, yes, we'll get three bouncy castles.'

'Last night I was dreaming about a shark on roller skates. He could skate, but he crashed into the door and went bang and then he crashed over there, into that, and he went inside and came out of one of those drawers like a square circle.'

'You have great dreams. I wish I had dreams like yours.'

'And he went racing round on his skates and went into the wall and one of his skates came off and...'

'He sounds like a fantastic skater.'

'He was. I didn't even know sharks could skate. When's Mummy coming?'

'She won't be long. She phoned and said she'd be coming soon. Here, I made some sandwiches. Have a sandwich.'

Roger places two plates on the breakfast bar, one with two sandwiches, the other with four.

Jimmy sits down and lifts a sandwich. He stares at the meat then puts the sandwich back on the plate.

'What happens when people die?'

'They go away.'

'Yes, but where do they go?'

'Away. Some place. Heaven. They go and live somewhere up in the clouds.'

'Then what do they do?'

'I don't know. It's a secret. No one knows.'

'Why is it a secret?'

'Why? Because no one's told us. Because if we knew, then... then it wouldn't be a secret and there'd be no point to anything and there'd be nothing to wonder about.'

'It's getting darker.'

'Where?'

'Outside. Look. It's getting darker. Even when we don't look, it gets darker.'

'Not to worry. Maybe it'll come light again. After the darkness, maybe it'll come light.'

'It might even snow. Do you think it might even snow?'

'No. I can safely say it's not even going to snow.'

'If it snowed I could lie on the floor and make an angel. Are *you* going to die?'

'Hopefully not too soon. Now eat your sandwich.'

'Will *I* die?'

'Why don't we talk about something else?'

'There's people I never see any more and Mum says he might as well be dead.'

'There's people I don't see, but that doesn't mean… There's plenty of people in the world I've never seen. Hey, sometimes you hear from people, out of the blue, unexpectedly, and that's a nice surprise. You never know.'

'This is ham. I don't like ham. Is ham like lamb? It sounds like lamb?'

'You do like ham. Your mother bought it for you. Yesterday you ate half the packet.'

'Yes, but I'm scared of crocodiles.'

'There's no crocodiles here. There's none for a hundred miles, two hundred. They're in zoos, behind bars.'

'But they scare me. I keep seeing them.'

'There's no crocodiles, I've told you.'

'I saw them on the telly.'

'They're in Africa. Africa's a long way away.'

'But I can't stop thinking about them. Every time I close my eyes I see crocodiles.'

'Well *don't* close your eyes.'

'Sometimes I have to close my eyes.'

'Yes. Sorry. I mean, now. You don't need to close your eyes now. It's not even dark.'

'But if I do close my eyes I think of crocodiles.'

'There's no crocodiles, not for thousands of miles. Honestly. No crocodiles will get you. I'm here. Your mother's here.'

'If we get three bouncy castles then we can have one each.'

'Yes.'

'And we can see who can bounce the highest.'

'It'll be you. You'll win that one. I know.'

'Do crocodiles live in zoos?'

'Yes. But there's no zoo near here. Honestly. You don't need to worry about crocodiles.'

'Simon has a pet crocodile.'

'No one has a pet crocodile.'

'Simon does. He told me.'

'Simon probably makes things up.'

'He said the crocodile lives in his garden. He said to run in zig zags, if it chases you, you run in zig zags.'

'Do you want to do something? While we wait for your mother. We can make something.'

Roger stands up and goes over to the window. He looks left, towards the brick wall. He thinks one day maybe he'll try and scale that damn wall, maybe see what's over the other side. As he stares at the bricks a taxi draws to a halt outside the house.

'Here, look, your mother. I told you she'd be back, didn't I?'

Part Two

8.00 p.m.

Mag is lounging on the sofa, feet up, eating from a bowl with her finger. Candles on the mantelpiece, candles on the table, open bottle of wine on the fireplace. Roger enters and walks towards the mirror. He's wearing dark trousers, a white cotton shirt, a dark jacket. He straightens the collar, wets his fingers and dabs at his hair.

Mag takes a sip of wine and points with her toes.

'I poured you one. Asleep?'

'Aye. He's gone.'

Roger runs his fingers over his lips, steps back, looks at himself, then steps forward again.

'What's that?'

'What's what?'

'That. You did a sort of wiggle.'

'It wasn't a wiggle. It's the way I walk.'

'Were you dancing?'

'Dancing. No. I can assure you.'

'Are you certain? I thought you were about to burst into a song and dance.'

'No. No dancing. So. At least you were looking at me. That's something I should take heart in.'

'I think so.'

'You only think so?'

'Maybe I got distracted. I want to eat with you. You want some of this?'

'What is it?'

Mag tilts the bowl toward Roger.

'Avocado.'

'Do we eat it?'

'You'll like it. It's very soft and very very wet.'

Roger turns and studies himself in the mirror. He appears nervous. Checking his shirt and jacket, his hair. He turns and for some form of reassurance looks at Mag. Mag licks her finger then speaks.

'I spy with my little eye something beginning with gun.'

'Can you see it?'

'I suppose it could be something else.'

Roger takes the gun from his hip and pushes it down the back of his trousers.

'How about this?'

Roger holds his arms out wide.

'Now you're being ridiculous. What were you like when you were a kid? Were you just the same?'

Roger shrugs then places the gun round his hip again.

'I was smaller.'

'You're a very funny man. Hey, you know, you look tired.'

'It feels like I've been awake for a thousand years.'

'What are you thinking about?'

'Nothing. Everything. Getting out of here. I'm thinking that if we get through tonight then everything will be okay and life will be normal.'

'Are you thinking about me?'

'I don't need to think about you.'

'I like that.'

'I stole it.'

'It doesn't matter. Do you want some food?'

'I'll not eat till it's done.'

'Why don't you do one of those wiggles again.'

'I didn't wiggle.'

'Yes you did. Come on. Move those old hips of yours. You need to get in shape.'

'I've got all the shape I need.'

'A little toning won't go amiss. Come over here. I've got terrible aches.'

Roger sits down on the sofa and pulls Mag's feet onto his lap. Mag takes a sip of wine as Roger massages her soles.

'Listen. You were late.'

'I phoned.'

'Yes, but you were late. Did you forget?'

'The clock stopped. I kept thinking time was going slow, then I realised the clock had stopped. It was three o'clock. It'd stopped dead on three o'clock.'

'It's important to have everything right. I told you, we fuck this up and that's it.'

'I said I was sorry and I said I'd never forget again. Here, try some.'

Mag holds out her finger to Roger but he ignores her and stands up.

'You never used to wear so much make-up. What's getting into you?'

'I did. I always did. Nothing's changed. Maybe you just never noticed.'

Mag sits up.

'Hey, come on, let's not do this. Thanks. I mean. For all this. I don't know what we would have done.'

'Something.'

'No. Nothing.'

'You would have coped.'

'And tomorrow we'll live off the fat of the land. There's wine if you want.'

'You seem remarkably calm.'

'I have ultimate faith in you. You're my saviour.'

'And what if this…?'

'Never.'

'It's been a long time.'

'But it's just this one thing isn't it? It's all very simple.'

'No. It's not simple.'

Roger takes a pack of cards from his breast pocket and shuffles them.

'Pick a card. Any card.'

'The queen of hearts.'

'I mean take one from the pack.'

'I did, last time, and you gave me the queen of hearts.'

'Yes, but this time it might be different.'

'What if it's the queen of hearts?'

'It doesn't matter. You take a card and I'll tell you which it is.'

'It's either a trick, or it's…'

'What?'

'Or it's a great deal of hope. But you know. You always know which it is.'

'No, I don't. That's the thing.'

'Is it magic, or is it a trick?'

Roger splays the cards again but drops them on the floor.

'Sorry. Sorry.' He almost breaks down into tears.

Roger bends down and picks up the cards.

'I told you you were tired.'

The lights flicker on then off.

'It's been like that all day,' says Roger. 'Listen. How are my hands?'

'Shaking.'

Roger looks at his watch.

'I need to go.' He points to the door. 'Keep it locked.'

'Okay.'

Roger kisses Mag then leaves the room without looking back. As he closes the door Mag peers over the sofa and speaks.

'Hey. I'll be thinking of you.'

Part Three

It's early morning. The lights of the room flicker on then off. After a moment they come on again and this time they stay on. We find Roger slumped on the floor against the sofa. He holds a blood-drenched towel over his wound. Jimmy is sitting on the hoover, still in his pyjamas. He appears oblivious to Roger's injury.

Jimmy speaks.

'I was dreaming about the house falling down. The wall over there, that one, was sinking and we had to put bricks underneath. We kept digging holes and filling them with bricks but it wasn't really falling down, it was just a dream. Why does it tickle when you lick the telly?'

Roger has the strength to talk and tries hard to keep Jimmy's spirit.

'Now there's an admission. Jimmy, kid, please. Don't lick the telly. It's not good for you.'

'Simon lives with his auntie. He said his mother kept forgetting to feed him so he went to live with his auntie.'

'I don't think that's true. His mother probably did feed him. I think Simon sounds like he likes to pull the truth.'

'He said she kept forgetting and he was hungry, so he went to live with his aunt. He sits next to me but he keeps getting into trouble.'

'They probably put him next to you so you can be a good influence.'

'Sometimes he stops me working. He flicks my ears.'

Jimmy stands up, goes to the sofa, kneels on the cushion and looks over the back.

'Why don't we make something with these boxes?'

'Maybe later.'

'I wanted to make a rocket. Can we make that rocket?'

'Of course we can.'

'Can we make two? One for me and one for you.'

'We'll see.'

'And some controls, can we put some controls inside?'

'Dials, levers, steering wheel, everything. You name it.'

'Do you want an apple?'

'I'm not hungry. But thanks. That's very nice of you.'

'Apples don't fill you. I didn't mean instead of proper food. It was just a… a…'

'An appetiser.'

'Yes.'

Roger winces as he pushes himself up against the sofa.

'Would *you* like an apple?'

'Is it a red or a green apple?'

'Why?'

'I don't like green apples. Big red ones, yes. But green ones, no. We could count to a thousand if you like.'

'And then what?'

Jimmy goes to the window and looks along the street.

'Emergency. Emergency. Quick. There's been a crash, look. It must have just happened. See that lorry, it's pushed that car off the road. There's some tyre marks, it must have gone screech, crash. And there's blood out there.'

'There'll be police any moment.'

'What happens if the police crash?'

'Then another police car comes to see.'

'What if all the police cars crash? Who comes then?'

'That's a good point. They might not have thought of that. Maybe they have some in reserve.'

'Or maybe a helicopter.'

'Maybe.'

'Or a hovercraft, or a boat.'

'I don't think they'd get a boat down here.'

'Or maybe bikes.'

'They'd get bikes here, yes.'

Jimmy looks one way then the other along the street.

'Where's the police? How come they've not come to the rescue?'

'It takes them a while. They have to drive from the station.'

'Nee naw, nee naw. Shhh, listen, if we're quiet, then we might be able to hear them. We had a pancake race yesterday, at school. Mine flew off in the wind. They weren't real pancakes, we drew them. Lucy's went over the fence and into the road and a truck ran over it but she drew another.'

'And you got yours back?'

'Mine was just by the grid. You used to have a car with a tyre on the top.'

'I did. How did you know that?'

'You told me. You said it was green, a big one, one with a tyre on the top. If we painted flames on Mum's car, them cars with big flames, well, they don't always come first, do they? Big flames on the side doesn't mean it'll be fastest.'

'That's right. Listen. Could you do me a big favour and get me a drink, please?'

Jimmy sits on the hoover.

'I could go on this.'

'Don't sit on the hoover.'

'It's a rocket. I'm going to the moon.'

Roger manages a smile and then sits for a while, watching Jimmy.

'Hey, spaceman. Tell me. What's it like up there?'

'There's no face. People say there's a face but there's no face. I wouldn't go if there was a face.'

'Can you see us?'

'I'm waving at you. Can you see me?'

'I can see you. Hey, little boy in the rocket, up there in the sky, can you see me waving at you?'

'Hello. I'm a busy astronaut. I'm going to the moon. How can a dish run away with a spoon? That's silly. Spoons don't run away.'

'It's just a rhyme. It doesn't really mean anything. Don't let it worry you. Jimmy, listen, that drink.'

Jimmy gets off the hoover and walks to the sink. He fills a glass with water and takes a sip. He places the glass on the draining board and lifts up a bottle of vinegar.

'Simon's dad drinks vinegar. He shakes the bottle into his mouth, just like this.'

With the lid closed, Jimmy shakes the bottle over his mouth.

'Would you like some vinegar?'

'No. Thank you. But water would be nice.'

Jimmy places the vinegar down and lifts the glass of water.

'I did a poster of Jesus at school and he was drinking vinegar, too. He had his arms tied and someone had to help him.'

'It wakes people. It's like a smelling salt.'

Jimmy places the glass of water by Roger's side. He strokes Roger's shoulder then goes back to the window.

'How come I never knew my father? I must have done something very bad. What did I do?'

'You did nothing. Honestly, son. You did nothing.'

'There must be lots of full buses and trains around.'

'Yes.'

'Should I go upstairs?'

'No. No. Please. Don't go upstairs. You have to stay down here. Even…listen.'

Roger sits forward, he's in severe pain.

'It's a game, and there's no going upstairs, do you understand?'

'But what if…?'

'There was a crocodile, under your bed. It can't get down the stairs but don't go up there, do you understand?'

'You said they were in Africa.'

'They are. They are in Africa. But maybe it was Simon's. It must have got out from his garden and maybe it got under your bed.'

Roger leans back into the sofa and coughs. He presses the towel to his side and breathes very slowly. He becomes very still and in the room there is silence.

'You look like you're trying to be a statue.'

'I am. I am trying.'

'You're very good at it.'

'Thank you.'

Roger is now almost prone. His arms stretch out to both sides, head and shoulders against the arm of the sofa. His feet cross at the ankles.

'Would you be my father?'

'Of course I'll be your father.'

'You won't go, will you?'

'No. I won't go.'

'When I grow up I want to be like you.'

'Listen. When you grow up, promise me, just be good.'

'Would you like me to sing a song? We did one at school.'

'I'd like that very much.'

'Okay. Are you ready?'

'Yes, I'm ready. Nice and loud.'

Jimmy looks at Roger and after a moment he smiles and begins to sing.

One more step along the world I go...
One more step along the world I go
From the old things to the new
Keep me travelling along with you

And it's from the old I travel to the new
Keep me travelling along with you

Round the corners of the world I turn
More and more about the world I learn
And the new things that I see
You'll be looking at along with me

And it's from the old I travel to the new
Keep me travelling along with you

As I travel through the bad and good
Keep me travelling the way I should
Where I see no way to go
You'll be telling me the way to go

And it's from the old I travel to the new
Keep me travelling along with you
Give me courage when the world is rough
Keep me loving though the world is tough
Leap and sing in all I do
Keep me travelling along with you

And it's from the old I travel to the new
Keep me travelling along with you

You are older than the world can be
You are younger than the life in me
Ever old and ever new
Keep me travelling along with you

And it's from the old I travel to the new
Keep me travelling along with you

The lights in the room flicker on and off.

So Long

I was arguing with my wife about promotion. She'd received an email from an ex-employer, asking if she'd like to apply for a post which had recently become available. It would have been a big step for her, moving up to head a department. She told me about the email and I was trying my hardest to encourage her to apply. We were sitting side by side on the sofa, drinking a bottle of wine and neither of us had eaten an evening meal.

'It's an ideal opportunity,' I said.

She wasn't convinced. She said it's not what she wanted to do, that it's a job doomed to failure.

'Why do I want to fail?' she said.

I topped up our glasses and we continued going over the possibilities. They said she could job-share and I pointed out that she could work fewer hours for more money.

'Just think,' I said.

'I am thinking,' she said.

'I mean, about the possibilities.'

We drank some wine and I considered making food but we were talking and it didn't feel right to leave and stand in the kitchen on my own, cooking.

At one point there was a large and long silence between us and I had a distinct feeling of separation.

'You know something?' she said. 'You no longer look like you and I no longer look like me.'

We finished the wine and went to bed.

Sometimes, when she lies with her back toward me, I think about how life used to be. Once, you couldn't get a razor between us. Now, everything seems like a long time ago and I wonder if her body was speaking to me in hieroglyphics.

In the night, I couldn't sleep and I blamed the lack of food for my incapacity to let myself drift away. It's strange, this growing apart together. One minute we forget to eat and the next we're saying goodbye.

As I lay awake I wonder about where to begin and where to end. All, of course, takes me no further forward, no further sideways, backwards, up or down.

'You have a particular way of seeing things,' she said to me.

We'd been talking and most of the time interrupting what each other was saying. I'd get halfway through a sentence and she'd interrupt, she'd get halfway through a sentence and I'd interrupt. It was almost a competition to see who could perform the fastest interruption.

Someday, some of this might make sense, or, might not make sense. Either way, we'll speak in languages other than this. We'll talk and listen and lie and cheat, we'll destroy what was good and we'll hope and pray for something better.

I watched from the window as she walked along the road, suitcase in hand. One time, she would have looked over her shoulder and would have waved and I would have returned the gesture and between us something would have been passed.

Instead. This is all I have.

Goodbye, my love.

Ice

It was six foot deep with snow. At least that's how it looked from the rear window. Maybe it wasn't as deep on the edge of the escarpment, but, still, it was deep, and that meant Helen was going nowhere.

Helen had been talking on the phone for almost an hour and by now she'd become weary.

'I told him. Yes. I know you told me not to, but I had to.'

And then.

'What? I think the line's cutting out. I can barely hear you. Lola? Lola?'

Helen placed the phone on the window sill and sat on the edge of the bed. It was almost noon.

Last week, Helen had been with Lola on a bus into town and they'd fallen out. Lola had not stopped talking about how life used to be, 'Before I gave up everything.'

By this she meant she given up on all the things she considered detrimental to her health. She'd stopped smoking and drinking. She'd stopped eating fatty foods. She'd put the TV into the skip next door had hired for renovations. The computer had gone, so too had the car.

Lola had been away for a short course on improving self-confidence, on improving lifestyle, on improving health.

'They're intrinsically interrelated,' said the smooth-talking forty-nine-year-old who ran the event.

'Look after this, and you will never look back,' he said as he tapped his heart.

Never Look Back was the company motto. They advised living each day as though it were your last. They asked for people to make each day better than the previous one. Give something else up, free yourself, release.

'Let go to live,' was another of Lola's newly acquired mantras.

'Let go of what?' Helen asked.

'Of everything. One thing, each day. I gave up the car and now go by bus, or walk, or by bike. I get lifts from people at work. I never knew Charlie. I mean, I spoke to him, but being in the car with him, well, we've talked. I'd never have done that. Don't you see? You should go on the course. It'll change your life.'

Lola even got rid of her books. Helen never

thought she would, but she called round one Saturday morning and there they were, all neatly placed in boxes.

'They came from charity, and they return to charity,' she said. 'Besides. There's always the library. What do I want to fill shelves with these for? I've read them all. Let someone else have the benefit.'

She sounded like a different woman from the one Helen had known from school. She tried to work out when and why she'd changed so much.

'You know, Lola, you can't give up on everything.'

Lola smiled at Helen and brushed the hair from her shoulder.

'I've never been so happy. It feels like every day I get to change, to find something new about the world. I can let go, I get lighter. Look.'

Lola smiled and opened her arms out wide.

Helen did look at Lola. And she couldn't deny that Lola looked good. Her skin was fresh and clear, her face bright, carefree.

'But what happens when you come to the end of everything?'

'In the end, there is nothing. You give nothing up, give nothing away. There's nothing left to give and nothing is all we have.'

Helen considered her smoking and drinking habits

and thought for a moment about whether to try to follow Lola's example.

'I'm not as strong as you. I need these, I need *things*.'

'I burned my photo albums. Some of these things, I mean, before you do it, you think, you wonder and you question, but then when it's done it's done.'

Lola and Helen had been trying to organise a break away together. They'd shopped around on the internet and in travel shops and each had made a list of three places they'd like to visit. Lola listed Prague, Rome and Paris. Helen listed the Gorges du Verdon, the Rhine Valley and the Isle of Skye. They spent a weekend being very pleasant to each other, saying how they didn't mind doing what the other wanted, but when it finally came to making a decision they finished up putting the places in a hat and asking Lola's neighbour to pull one out. The resulting trip was to Rome.

They provisionally booked the holiday but when it loomed Helen started to have doubts and used an out-of-date passport excuse.

Their relationship cooled and for a month or two they didn't speak. Finally, Helen left a message on Lola's answer machine and they got together again and spoke of how ridiculous they'd been.

'Nothing is worth it,' said Lola.

'We'll be together forever. Friends for always.'

Lola smiled and kissed Helen on the cheek.

★

'I want to go south,' said Lola. 'Somewhere where it's warm.'

'I like the snow,' said Helen. 'I like it when the snow arrives silent in the night, then when you open the curtains the world is different. Out comes the sun and by noon all the snow has gone. Isn't that just amazing?'

'This isn't going anywhere.'

'It's getting deeper. Can you give up loving snow?'

The two women had a mutual friend, Simon, who died last year from a prolonged illness. He was buried in Canada and they talked now and again of going to visit his mother to tell her some of the stories of his life. It was another of the trips they'd discussed but had never got round to fully organising. Lola still believed they would do some of these things, the weekend away, the trip to Canada, the boat along the Nile and so on, but recently, Helen had realised they would never do these together. She looked out over the snow and knew, at that moment, that she would live for the rest of her life in this same small house and that she would always be alone. The thought came to her as a shudder, but, soon after, she felt a sense of calm, of acceptance.

'If I lived my life over again, who would I become?'

Later that afternoon they played the *O Game*.

Helen had found the thing in the loft and had brought it down into the kitchen.

'See. Look. I told you we had a copy.'

The two of them went through the pile of questions…

'Sometimes. Yes. Of course. Lots of times. Lots of times. Lots of times.'

Lola showed Helen the scar on her back from the time she'd been caught in a net. They talked about love and dependency.

'I'll always be alone,' said Helen.

★

Simon had a brief relationship with Lola. She'd worked hard on him, calling round, phoning, buying him gifts. She engineered meetings and though initially he said he wasn't interested, her persistence won him over. They spent a weekend holed up in his house by the lake and she'd lavished him with attention. He was a man of routine, woke early, went for a swim, and exercised in the garden under the elm tree. The view from his veranda was spectacular. Most mornings the lake was covered with a fine low-lying mist and he'd sit and watch as the mist slowly dispersed. Simon's house was the only one by the lake, a mile or so away was a small hut, but that was only used by one or two fishermen.

On Sunday afternoon Simon and Lola argued and that was the last of the two of them being *an item*. They remained good friends and neither of them showed interest in trying to rekindle their fling. Helen though, had always loved Simon. She never let Simon know about her feelings, never showed him any attention other than that a friend would show. She told Lola and the next she knew, Lola and Simon were together.

'I knew it wouldn't work out,' said Lola. 'We were sexually incompatible.'

Helen listened to Lola comb over the details of the brief fling and she understood the word jealousy. After Simon died the house by the lake was sold. The developer demolished the house prior to gaining planning permission and had gone ahead with the rapid destruction of the property. Permission for the development was never agreed and so the only option for the developer was to re-build the house exactly as it was. The developer refused and so the site was left empty. Brick and slates were sold or pilfered and over the two years since his death weeds and grass had grown over the foundations. In the snow, nothing of the former house could be seen.

'Water can be so cruel,' said Helen.

'I remember Simon walking onto the frozen lake. Do you remember? He was treading out, thinking he'd fall through any minute. There was that big crack, that sound echoing round the lake. Remember? He came slipping and sliding back to the bank, his heart thumping. We laughed, can you remember?'

'I wanted him to fall in. Not to drown, but to slip in so we'd have to rescue him.'

'We should go to Canada, show his mother the films.'

'We were young, weren't we. Now, I just feel old.'

'Why don't we do something together, maybe take a walk in the snow, out to the lake?'

★

When it came to it, Lola decided to stay and make the fire.

'I'll make a big pot of stew,' she said. 'I realised

yesterday where I'd gone wrong. I'd been looking for a wallet and not a husband. It took me thirty years to come to that. Silly, isn't it?'

Helen went down to the lake by herself and when she got there the water was frozen over. She looked around for the remains of the house but the snow had covered it and she'd even forgotten exactly where the building used to be.

The lake and forest were silent and after a moment she walked out onto the ice. At first, she stepped carefully, but then, after a moment she felt more at ease, more secure and she edged out towards the middle of the lake. There, she stopped and looked down through the ice. Down there, in the water, she could see fish swimming. One came up to the circle she'd rubbed in the ice and appeared to look right at her.

As the stew simmered away, Lola was sure she heard an echo.

*

An hour later than expected Helen came in through the door, soaked, shivering, smiling.

'I was on the lake, on the ice, and you know, I almost drowned. Can you believe it, me, not swimming, not trying? I almost drowned. I wasn't even trying to save myself. I walked out to the middle and when the ice cracked I just let myself slip down into the water. I was there, still, and I looked up and could see the sun through the ice. I could see it, glowing. I am alive, Lola. I'm alive.'

Birdsong

Last night I was awake for an hour or more. At one point I looked at the clock and it was 4.22. I tried to let my mind be as still as possible but I couldn't stop whatever was in there from racing.

I'd been reading an art book, a book of workings and jottings, a book of studio notes, doodles and ideas. On the first page it said, *big gates move on small hinges.*

The book was filled with people trying to get at the essence of what they wanted to say. Lots of struggle and fight, plenty of imagination. But what stayed in my mind was just a few simple words.

Big gates move on small hinges.

My wife was sleeping and every so often her breathing made a tiny whistling sound. We'd been through paper and wood, copper and tin, all those days of giving and receiving, and I don't think I'd ever heard that sound before.

Yesterday afternoon I was working with a group of wonderful people I'd known for thirty weeks. One of them told a story about someone he knew getting the sack from work for stopping to urinate in the woods. Two young girls saw him, reported the incident, and that was that, the man was sacked.

Pretty soon someone was saying about how a man in Turkey was caught with a goat and as punishment the village made him marry the beast. Another said how a man in Brazil was arrested for making love to a pavement.

The jokes came thick and fast.

'Maybe he was just laying the slabs.'

'Oh. He *used* me then walked all over me.'

The jokes got worse till someone mentioned mental health issues and the laughter soon ceased.

'What would it take to be reduced to having sex with a pavement?' she said. 'Is that really all that funny?'

I talked about dancing, about how a very good dancer might be able to do Irish, tap, jazz, Morris, any type of dancing, and that the dancing might hold our attention, and with luck, elevate us to some new and wondrous place. And what if there were a few dropped steps, some slight timing issues? Would it really matter? Need we be perfect?

We talked dance until someone said, 'Are we really here to talk about dancing?'

I thought about shoehorns, about whether we need them for old shoes as well as the new. New ideas, I thought, they take some getting into.

So we talked about characters as films and I asked for people to think of a film, a scene, something, anything.

It caused uproar and I thought of new ideas, of blisters.

We'd been reading a short story by Richard Brautigan and when we finished someone asked, 'Did he write it while he was still alive?'

Of course, it seemed ridiculous until I thought it through.

Sparks flew, ideas were exchanged and all at once we were alive to it all.

I thanked Richard Brautigan for bringing electricity to places it had never before been.

The power comes from not describing the thing as it is but from the thing as something else. *Make it new.*

My wife's newfound wheeze faded and I was left with sounds of the skylark and song thrush.

This morning I decided to find out what the birds were trying to say.

It's the clarity, the purity of dawn air, the stillness

that makes the birdsong more distinct. They say the same message, over and over, in a multitude of ways.

Keep away, keep away. Come here, come here. Keep away, keep away. Come here, come here.

At one point my wife and I talked about self-deception.

'It's about evolution, about self-defence, something else sends an instant reaction through us, but ourselves, no, we can't do it quickly enough, the brain knows we are doing it so it can't be surprised by itself, it can't catch itself unawares, it can't trick itself into thinking it's under attack from itself.'

After that came a long period of silence.

In a jar in the kitchen we keep a whole load of scraps of paper. Written on each one is a different thing. *When were you happy? What happened last week? What is important? What are you going to do? Who is to blame?*

It was my wife's idea. She spent an evening writing out all these sentences and every so often she'd dip in her hand and we'd talk about what it said. She said we were becoming stuck, that we were running out of things to say to each other.

Sometimes we'd be sitting in the kitchen and she couldn't bear it. So, she came up with this notion of having randomly organised discussions.

What did you dream about? When did you last cry? What is the colour of May Day?

I've no idea if we'd been through the whole lot of them. She wrote them out without me seeing. Sometimes we discussed the same thing three or four times but each time the outcome had been different.

Last night, she pulled out a slip of paper and it said: *Why don't you leave?*

'Because I don't want to,' I said.

For a while she stayed still. Then she folded the paper and dropped it back into the jar.

'And you?' I asked.

'And me?'

'Yes. And you.'

The films that people came up with were *The Wizard of Oz*, *Carry on Laughing*, *Jaws*, *Singing in the Rain*...

'You mean you want me to talk about the film?'

'Yes.'

'How can I describe her by talking about a film? Do I choose a scene, do I talk about the actress, saying, *She looks like Marilyn Monroe?*'

My wife told me the skylark never repeats itself.

It must have been after three in the morning when I realised I was awake and not in a dream. All at once the birds began and I wondered about their songs. I'd heard and not heard them before and I felt lucky to be alive.

I was lucky to be alive but was very very alone.

How could I name them, remember them, describe their song?

'What do you mean never repeats? Never?'

'Well you can listen for hours and it'll never sing the same song.'

Is that difficult to believe?

There's a radio station that plays bird songs. The station, I think, is called *Birdsong*.

I remember she said to me, 'It's a good idea, but do you think it's on a loop? I mean, if it repeats, say after half an hour, or a day, or a week, or a year.'

'Would it matter?'

'Yes. Of course. I'd feel cheated. If it was all on a loop it wouldn't be the same.'

By then she was fast asleep and the birds had been singing for half an hour or more.

I kept drifting in and out of ideas, trying to remain with the song but finding myself all over again with memories of when we first met, of us together, dancing.

How can I describe an ending when it's so near?

Don't tell us what it is. *Make it new.*

Come closer, come closer.

Somehow I was onto thinking about that and I caught myself and thought, what am I doing, why not listen to the birds? *Go back, go back.*

Was it really going back or was it moving forward?

Come here, come here. Keep away, keep away.

Even the skylark sends mixed messages.

Then someone says, 'You know, I think I understand what you mean. By God. I think I've got it.'

Love Of Fate

The little boy was sitting at the end of the table and the man was by his side, helping him with his food. Carefully, the boy placed down his knife and fork.

'Tell me something funny,' he said.

The man thought for a moment then smiled.

'I was out the other night and I asked for a pitcher of water. The waiter brought me a photo of the Atlantic Ocean.'

'I don't understand,' said the boy. 'And how come you get more food than me?'

'I'm bigger than you, as is your mother. We need more fuel inside us. You're bigger than the dog, so you get more fuel than her. It's a size thing.'

The boy cleared his throat and straightened his knife and fork.

'I think I've had enough to eat now. Can we finish the rocket?'

'But you've barely touched it. Just one more mouthful.'

'One more will make my head hurt.'

'Then do you want something else?'

'Did you say you had choc-ices?'

'I did. But not unless you eat some more of that.'

'But choc-ices make my headache go away.'

The man stood up and scraped the remains from one plate to the other. Then, he took the plates and the cutlery through to the kitchen. He filled two glasses with water and returned.

'Your mother said she smelled gas this morning. Did you smell gas?'

'What's gas?'

'It goes underground, for fires, for fuel, for heating. It's in pipes. You can't see it, it's underground.'

'Do trees use gas?'

'No. Trees drink water.'

The man placed the drinks on the table and took his seat.

'And that's underground,' said the boy. 'You told me once there's a table under the ground, and trees have roots that drink water from the table.'

The boy took a sip of his drink.

'Sort of. Yes. Did I tell you that?'

The man glanced out of the window. It was evening. Over the road, above the houses, the sky had turned orange-red.

'Maybe it was a fire, maybe your mother smelt a fire. Sometimes you can smell things from a long long way away.'

The boy sniffed and smiled.

'I can smell Australia.'

'Now that *is* a long way away.'

'It smells like an ostrich.'

'What do I smell like?'

'You smell like, like a truck that's tipping out sand.'

'That's great. You smell of, of…'

'A field with chocolate in.'

'You're too good at this game. I wish I had some of your imagination. You lose a lot when you grow old.'

The boy took a drink of water then gazed around the room.

'I spy with my little eye, something beginning with C.'

'Cloud.'

'No.'

'Car.'

'No.'

'Crayon.'

'No. It's a cement mixer. It went past the window. It's gone now. It's your turn.'

The man stroked his beard and looked back towards the window.

'I spy with my little eye, something beginning with T.'

'Train.'

'Nope.'

'Trampoline.'

'Now where's the trampoline?'

'In the back of that truck over the road.'

'How do you know?'

'There might be.'

'Yes, there might be, but it's not a trampoline.'

'Okay. It's a tree.'

'Yes. That's it. Well done. You're a very clever kid.'

'When will Mum be back?'

'She won't be long.'

'Yes. But when will she get here? You said she'd be back soon.'

'She will be.'

'Will she be drunk?'

'No. She'll be fine. Why not do another I spy?'

'I can't think of anything. Can I just sing?'

'Of course you can sing. You're very musical, I can tell.'

'Oh the grand old Duke of York, he had ten thousand ladders, he marched them up to the top of the hill and he marched them down again. And when they were up they were up, and when they were down they were down, and when they were only halfway up, they were neither up nor down.'

The man clapped his hands together and smiled.

'That's fantastic. I like ladders.'

'So do I. You didn't get me a choc-ice.'

'Did I say you could have one?'

'Yes.'

'Okay. I'll get you a choc-ice. Then let's finish that rocket.'

The man stood up again and brushed his hand over the boy's head.

'Are you leaving tonight?' said the boy. 'I saw you packed a suitcase. Are you leaving?'

'I might be. Yes. Probably. I will be. Why don't you sing another song? You've a good voice.'

'I don't know any more songs.'

'Me and your mother. Listen.'

'The first time you came you gave me an aeroplane.'

'Did I? Did I do that?'

'Yes. I hope her next boyfriend is like you.'

The man ruffled the boy's hair.

'He will be. Don't you worry. He will be.'

Acknowledgements

I was fortunate enough to receive a commission from the East Midlands Regional Reading Group Project to work on this collection of short stories. The commission stemmed from the *Writers2Readers* initiative, which brought together a number of writers and readers in the East Midlands. Meetings with reading groups in Shirebrook, Waddington, Kettering and Wollaton led to numerous developments in my approach to writing and the stories in this collection reflect my experiences.

I would like to thank the nine public library authorities in the East Midlands, the Museums and Libraries Archive East Midlands (MLA), The Reading Agency (TRA), and Arts Council England (East Midlands) for their input and support. Thanks goes to Priscilla Baily, Debbie Hicks and Alison Betteridge for their involvement. Thanks also to the reading groups generous enough to give their time and thoughts in discussions related to writing, reading and storytelling.

Special thanks to Paddy Fagan and Christine Plant for their enthusiasm and insight. Thanks also to Louise Rainbow and Jacek Laskowski for their positive approach, and a big thank you to Route for their generous advice, involvement and overview.

Jack and Sal
Anthony Cropper

ISBN 1 901927 21 0
Price UK - £8.95

Jack and Sal, two people drifting in and out of love. Jack searches for clues, for a pattern, for an explanation to life's events. Perhaps the answer is in evolution, in dopamine, in chaos theory, or maybe it can be found in the minutiae of domesticity where the majority of life's dramas unfold.

Here, Anthony Cropper has produced a delicately detailed account of a troubled relationship, with a series of micro-stories and incidents that recount the intimate lies, loves and lives of Jack and Sal and their close friend Paula.

'Here we have some really beautiful pieces. It is remarkable how he has mixed happiness and bitterness, love and cruelty, sadness with some hilarious parts, just like life does.'
Manuel Lafuente

'The underlying sadness of the doomed relationship is haunting. But that's good. That's the way it should be.'
Michael Lyng

Weatherman
Anthony Cropper

ISBN 1 901927 16 4
Price UK - £6.95

In this beautifully crafted first novel, Anthony Cropper skilfully draws a picture of life inextricably linked to the environment, the elements, and the ever changing weather.

Ken sits out the back, in the flatlands that surround Old Goole, and watches the weather. That's what he was doing with poor Lucy, that fateful day, sat on the roof of his house, lifting her up to the sky. Lucy's friend, Florrie, she knew what would happen.

All this is picked up by Alfie de Losinge's machine, which he had designed to control the weather. Instead, amongst the tiny atoms of cloud formations, he receives fragmentary images of events that slowly unfold to reveal a tender, and ultimately tragic, love story.

'Cropper's real talent is his narrative voice, which has an effortlessly energetic quality to it, one that conjures up in the mind's eye what the narrator must be doing, torso leaning from one side to another, and then looming forward as he makes a point.' Tom Bowden - Education Digest

Anthony Cropper

Anthony has published two novels
and has co-edited three collections of
short stories. His play, *I'll Tell You About
Love*, won the BBC Alfred Bradley
Award for Radio Drama. Anthony
lives by the side of the Trent and
teaches Creative Writing for the
University of Nottingham. He is
married with three sons and has a
dog named Spot.